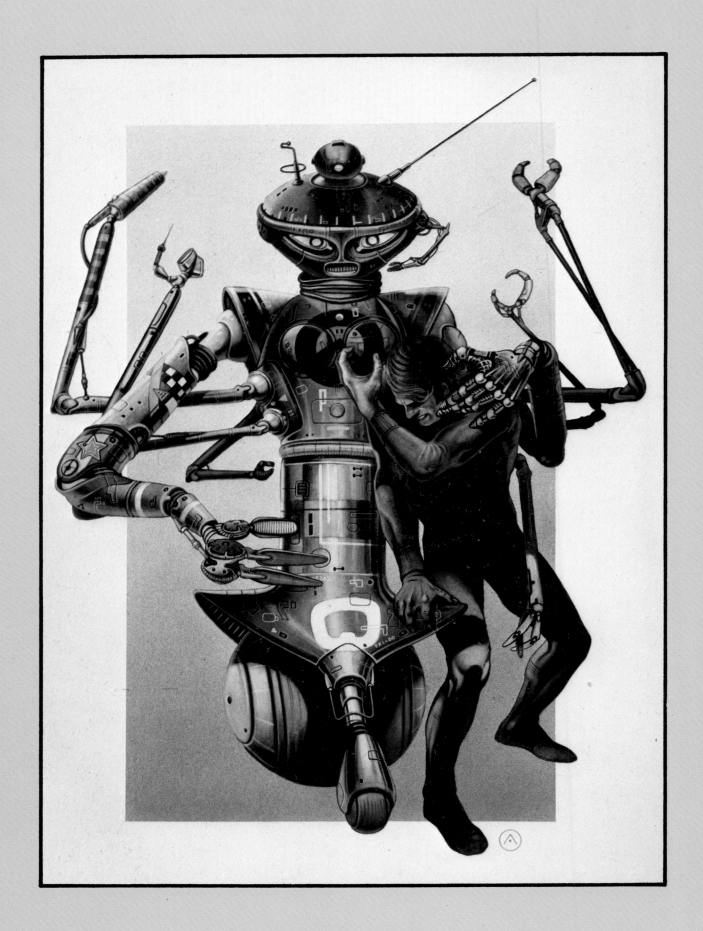

Monsters and Medics

Beauty and the Beast

A Collection of Heroic Fantasy Illustrations

CHRIS ACHILLEOS

A FIRESIDE BOOK
Published by
Simon and Schuster New York

Paper Tiger

Printed in Spain by
Printer Industria Grafica S.A.
Sant Vicenç dels Horts 1978
Deposito Legal B-22637-1978

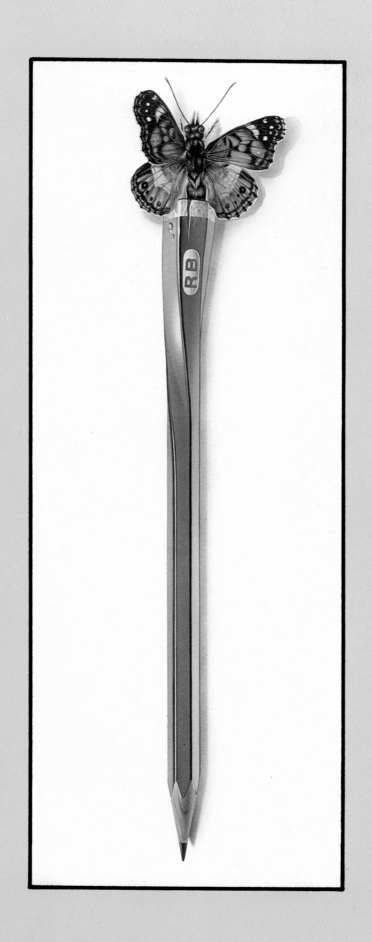

CHRIS ACHILLEOS

Chris Achilleos was born in Famagusta, Cyprus in 1947, but moved to England with his family in 1960. He went to school in London, then on to Hornsey College of Art in 1965, where he studied technical and scientific drawing. Since 1969 he has become a foremost fantasy illustrator, mainly of book jackets featuring science fiction and "Sword and Sorcery" tales. He lives in London and is married with two children.

Achilleos' fascination with popular heroic imagery dates from his childhood. He learned about Greek myth and legend from "Classic" comics while he lived in Cyprus, and moved on to the finely drawn and forceful strips in "Eagle" when he came to live in England. Frank Bellamy's outstanding "Eagle" centre-spread, "Heros the Spartan", was particularly influential on his growing interest in the possibilities of comic illustration.

While studying at Hornsey College of Art, he collected American comic imports, and absorbed the dynamism of their graphics into his own comic strip work. He mixed the technical control he gained from his main course of study with these influences to produce highly finished science fantasy designs, direct progressions from his childhood dreams and stimulae. These dreams were, and are, mainly of the heroes of the past; noble savages who fight by hand and sword against enormous odds, like Achilles, or Beowulf, or the new superhumans invented by such writers as Robert E. Howard in his "Conan" series.

Chris Achilleos brings a meticulous technical skill to the illustration of tales of bloody heroism. In his polished artwork, cold metal gleams against and mingles with strange fetishist clothing. On his warriors and Amazons, armour merges into skin and fur; jewelled pendants drip from highly crafted gold and silver bracelets, while ornate swords are strapped and buckled onto body-moulded carapaces.

His heroes hack victory from the hideous forms of semi-human adversaries. The worse the odds against these champions are, the more complete and gory their eventual triumph will be, echoing the presence of some dark, mysterious "rightness".

His combatants sweep from rocky amphitheatres to the depths of ghoul-infested caves. But their battles can have only one result — the hero with a bloody sword or axe will stand triumphantly astride a heap of dead or dying victims.

His heroine, meanwhile will merely stand or lie unmoved against this backdrop of barbaric carnage. Loaded with the trappings of eroticism, yet somehow cold, her image recurs in Achilleos' work as the symbol of an unattainable perfection. The heroine provides the reason for the hero's acts of maniac valour — her inaccessibility completes the mythic pattern of his world.

Achilleos' style is based on fastidious application. He works exclusively to commission, painting by daylight systematically and slowly, spending from one to four weeks on each picture. He draws from photographic and other visual source material, working the pictures up from pencil roughs and developing them in inks, watercolours and fabric dyes. To obtain the finish needed on his graphic work, he uses an airbrush; but for his large heroic pictures he uses acrylics on canvas, a medium he much prefers.

Though his commissions vary, there are three constant preoccupations in his work which he will freely admit to. His heroes are "born adventurers who live by their wits, instinctively fighting for the right without being aware of it". His beasts are usually humanoid, for "the most effective monster is something you can relate to". His women, finally, are even more large than life than his other creations; "Pure fantasy, as perfect as possible".

INDEX
Cover see P.61

9

The Holy Warrior—Muhammad Ali

Bruce Lee   My Martial Arts Training Guide.   (Jeet Kune-Do)

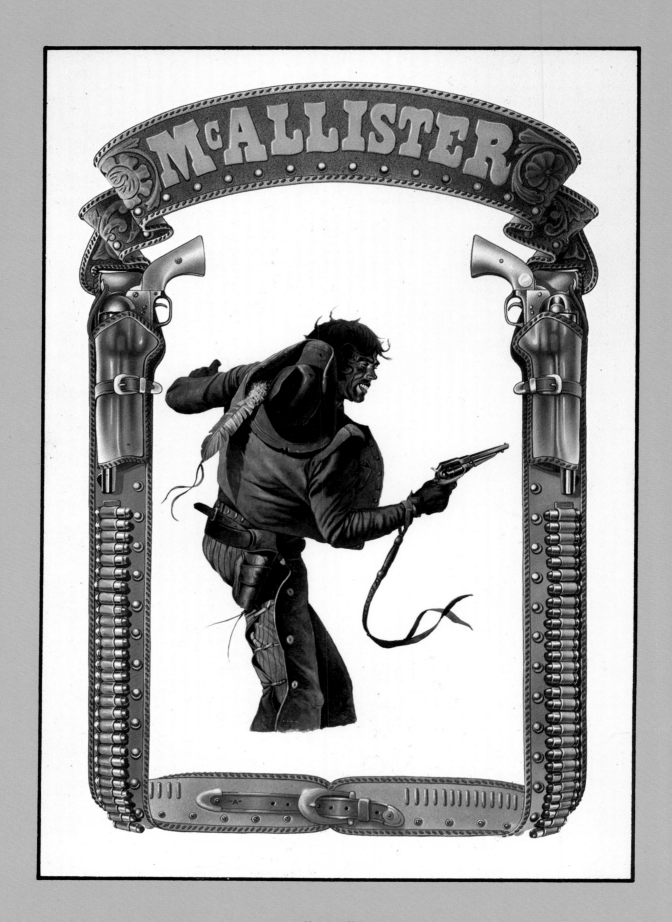

Kill McAllister

McAllister Justice

Rage of McAllister   McAllister series cover

The Hard Men   McAllister series cover

The unbidden

EVERYBODY LOVES A HERO

The time is out of joint. Behold: the Hero comes to set the clock aright.

★

Man lives forward, looks backward. The present is ever intolerable. *Now* — the moment of existence — is full of pangs and passions. "Tomorrow will be better — like the good old days."

★

From this contradiction, "the hero" arises: the hero is a model of the past bound to the present to create the future.

The hero is a paradigm of Time.

★

The hero is unique but not alien. He is singular not solitary. Even when abandoned and alone, shunned by his tribe, the hero cannot be solitary. For he contains the flower of his race and the seed of civilization within him. The hero is not primitive. He is primal. Think of Aeneas.

The hero emerges from the barbarous to destroy the barbarous. The first steps of the hero are away from the primordial ooze whence his race took birth. Thus Beowulf destroys Grendel and Grendel's dam. With all the barbarity of his race, Beowulf destroys the barbarousness that bedevils that race.

Beowulf fertilizes the ground with his victim's blood. The seed of civilization is sown. The seed is the action itself.

The hero cannot act once and be done with it. He must act again and again and again. The hero is an incomplete verb.

Beowulf slays the dragon but is slain himself. His tribe survives. He is dissolved in flames. This is the point of the hero: he is mortal. Everything that lives within him is, by its very nature, the epitome of his race and its destiny. His action is that destiny. When his tasks are fulfilled, his energy is absorbed by the race and he must vanish. He becomes a withered limb on the tree of his tribe. A monument. The tribe moves forward. The hero remains.

Heroes are always perceived in the past. There are no living heroes.

The hero is a verb whose action is complete.

★

The Greeks, who more than most generated heroes like sparks, considered that even for them the Age of Heroes was dead.

★

A courageous man who fights fiercely to defend his country is not a hero. He is a courageous man.

A hero defends the spirit of his race, acts singly and by his own will. He is condemned to be a hero. He cannot be drafted from the factory floor.

★

Ghengis Khan built a city of skulls.

★

Heroes are not humanitarians. They are racialists. They dash the infant brains of their enemies on the building blocks of their tribe.

★

The hero is eccentric, abnormal. He cannot be submerged in the masses. His gravity makes him rise. The spirit of his tribe is the centre of his individuality.

★

The hero has nothing to do with politics — just as politics has nothing to do with heroism.

★

The hero works *for* the race and *against* the masses. The masses retard, are retarded. "Hero of the Soviet Union" is a contradiction in terms.

★

Early heroes are confused with gods. "Great men have been among us: the gods walked in the marketplace." This is quite natural. Gods are made in the image of man, heroes in the image of gods: Horus, Osiris, Quetzalcoatl.

★

Later heroes are fully mature, their humanity greater and more moving than obscure godhead: Hector, King David, Cú Chulainn, Beowulf, Siegfried.

★

Mature heroes are mortals who die and are deified: Hercules, Castor and Pollux. King Arthur?

★

Heroes are human because they seek to be more than human.

★

It would seem that all legendary heroes are derived from actual historical figures — even the oldest of them, Gilgamesh.

★

Heroes emerge when a tribe is menaced or menaces. Triumph alone determines the virtue of the cause.

Heroes respond to menace.

★

A developing tribe needs menace. Menace hastens change.

★

Heroes arose late. Racial identity was long coming in human history. There were cavemen geniuses. There were no cavemen heroes.

★

Genuinely primitive societies have no heroes. Heroes are a symptom of change, the assertion of tribal domination and a demonstration of tribal superiority. By the time a hero appears, his tribe is already beyond the palisade of mere survival and brute simplicity. The hero is the Will of the tribe.

The hero is the historian who makes history.

★

Who are the heroes of the Eskimos?

★

Developed societies which resist change are deficient in heroes — the Egyptians, for example.

★

Heroes know nothing of morality. They deal with what-is. Heroic action is imposs-ible in the face of justice. Whatever heroes do, is correct. Heroes personify that "might is right". The most interesting acts of heroism occur when two heroes — the spirits of two races — clash: Hector and Achilles. David and Goliath. History goes to the victor. Morality is the jewel the defeated display.

★

Alexander the Great murdered his father. Who cares? Alexander is a hero.

★

Shakespeare describes Achilles as a cheat and a coward. Who cares? Achilles is a hero.

★

Heroes are more than brute, they are brain. They incarnate Man's rise above the animal. They are sly, wily, cunning. They are confidence men: they lie, bewilder, deceive. Ulysses. They must have their way, and so they make it.

Everything falls before the hero, or he is no hero. And we should not know his name.

★

Force and violence are cake and custard to the hero. Trickery is a sugar-plum.

★

The hero cannot exist apart from menace. Where there is none, he will make some. If Fafner did not exist, Siegfried would invent him.

Cú Chulainn did battle with the sea.

★

The hero requires that the world be a poison planet. There is no need for heroes in the Land of Milk and Honey.

The hero carouses with demons.

★

The hero chastens and hastens. He moves from birth to death in a smooth arc of terror, murder, deception and triumph. Out of his vice comes the virtue of his tribe.

★

Men need heroes more than heroes need men.

★

Societies in decay are bedevilled by heroes.

Third century Rome witnessed Emperors disguise themselves as Hercules, as if their mere appearance were not his 13th labour.

An obsession with heroes is the wound of spiritual and racial Eunuchism.

★

Report on the 20th Century:

Item 1: Heroes abound on football fields and prove all men equal. They wear and advertize "Brut", sign contracts for $2 million, have two children, central heating, and an album of press cuttings. Their heads are stacked at Madame Tussaud's. They speak poor English.

Item 2: Boy meets girl. Hero marries heroin.

Kuldesak   The Black Moon (volume 2 The Cabal) ➝

Almuric

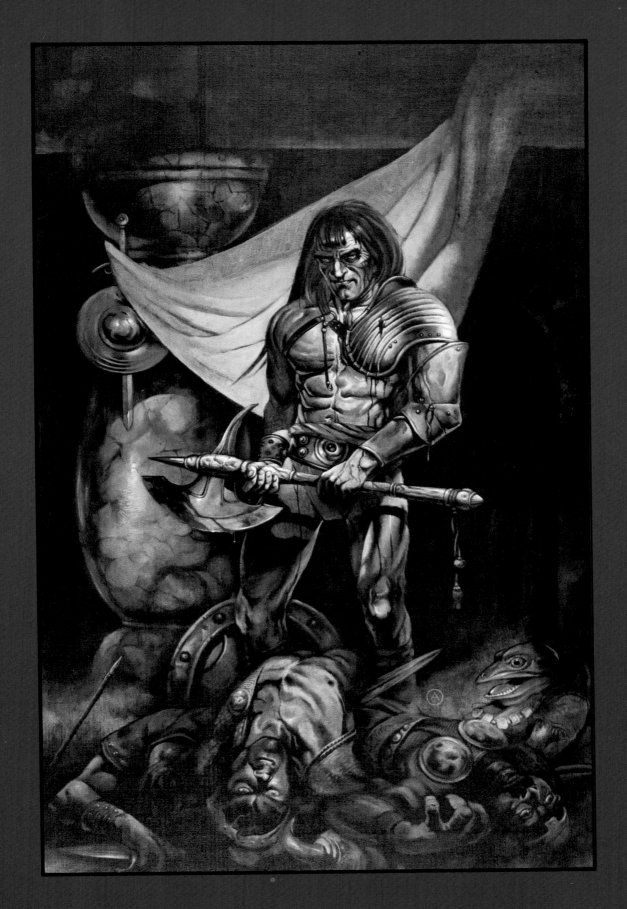

King Kull

The Bull and the Spear

The Shadow Kingdom

The Lost Valley of Iskander   Swords of Shahrazar
The World Set Free   A Story of the Days to Come

Chariots of Fire

Tanar of Pellucidar   Savage Pellucidar

Back to the Stone Age

32

Land of Terror

Darkness Weaves

Moorcock's Book of Martyrs

The Eve of Midsummer

The Strickland Demon

The Land Leviathan

Raven Book III A Frozen God

Tanith

Will O The Wisp

War of the Wing Men

Swordships of Scorpio

Transit to Scorpio

The Suns of Scorpio

Marauders of Gor

Hunters of Gor

Captive of Gor

Worms of the Earth

Warrior of Scorpio

Raiders of Gor

Nomads of Gor

Assassin of Gor

Raven Book II A Time of Ghosts

Raven

Raven Book I

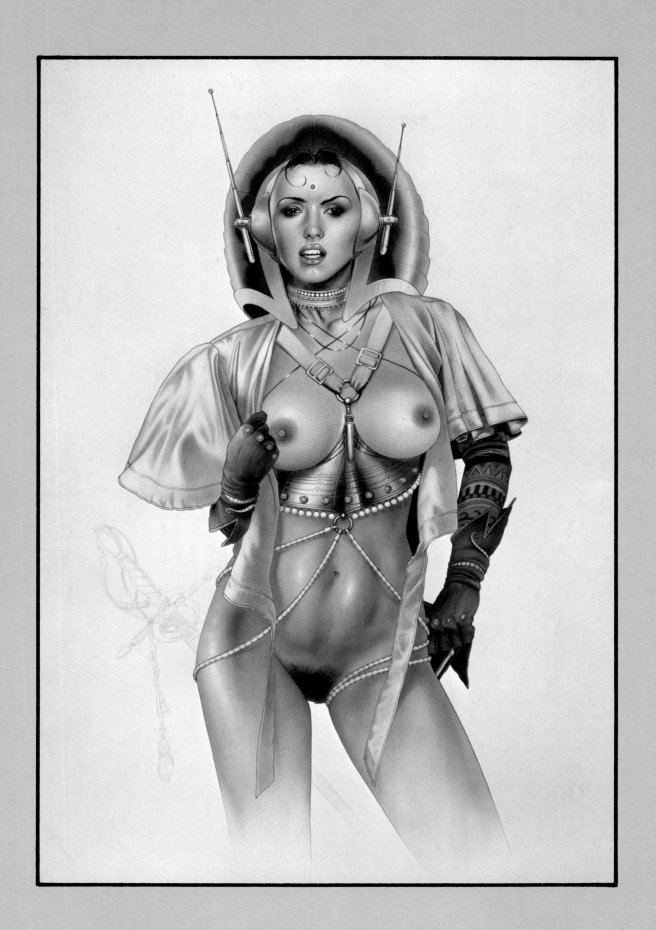

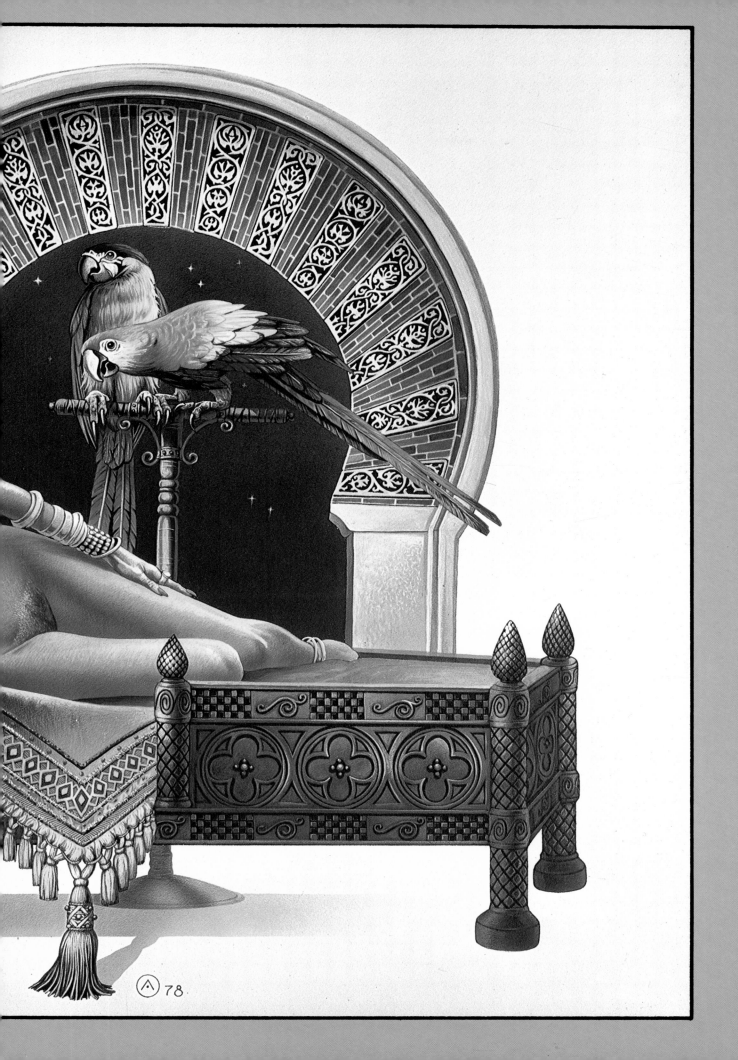

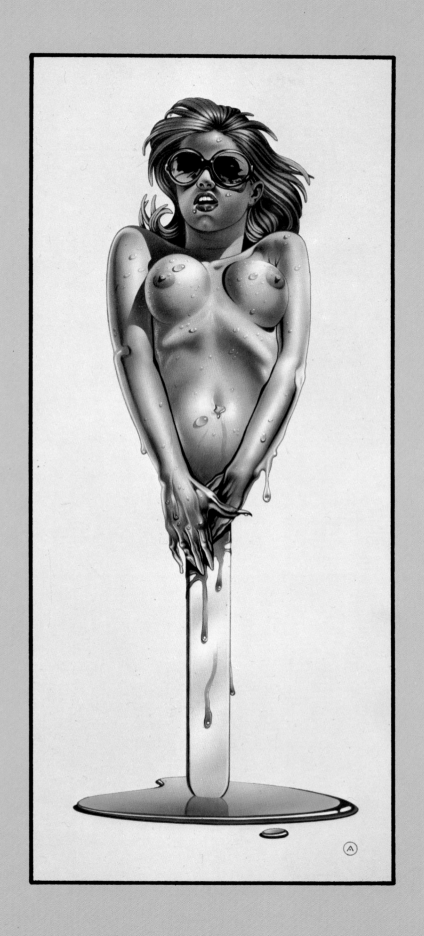

The Valley of the Worm

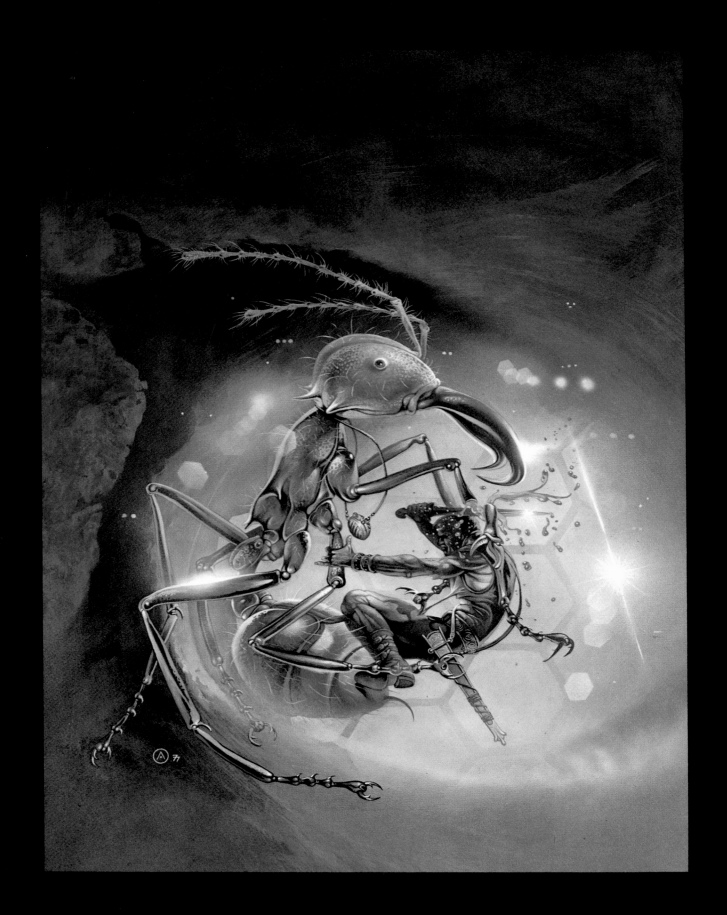

Priest Kings of Gor

Doctor Who and the Space War

Doctor Who and the Ark in Space   Doctor Who and the Dinosaur Invasion
Doctor Who and the Genesis of the Daleks   Doctor Who and the Glaws of Axos

The Doctor Who Monster Book I

Amok King of Legend